To Garrett Reese
From Grandma

Always be a friend!

Pat Bissonnette

Rescue at Wiseman's Pond

Patty Wiseman

Illustrations by
Syrena Seale

1209 South Main Street
PMB 126
Lindale, TX 75771

Illustrations by Syrena Seale
Cover Design by Syrena Seale
Book Design by Champagne Book Design

Library of Congress Control Number Data
Wiseman, Patty.
Rescue at Wiseman's Pond / Patty Wiseman.
[Color—Fiction   2. Animals—Fiction   3. Stories in rhyme]
Fiction. | BISAC: JUVENILE FICTION / Social Situations / Values. | JUVENILE FICTION / Animals / General. |
PCN 20179489942017
ISBN 978-1-940460-994

Pattywiseman.com
Bookliftoff.com

DEDICATION

This little book is dedicated to all my grandchildren
and great-grandchildren,
I love each and every one!

May you love one another;
May you work as a team.
Remember you are family,
A part of someone's dream

You are the future;
You come from our past.
Go forward together,
And you will be blessed

You are here for a reason;
Lessons to learn.
Together a beacon,
For others who yearn

Rescue at Wiseman's Pond

Daddy's shop is Ronnie's favorite place.

He works there because there's lots of space.

His dog Cutter hangs out there, too.

They are friends for life, through and through.

Today he will fix his bike;

Maybe later take Cutter for a hike,

But before he can twist the wrench,

Mrs. Barnswallow landed on the bench.

Ronnie laughed and Cutter barked.

Mrs. Barnswallow didn't think it was such a lark.

She swooped too close to Cutter's head.

She swooped again, and then she fled.

Ronnie smiled and went back to work.

But alas, this wasn't just a quirk.

She swooped again and flew back out.

Cutter went to see what it was all about.

Cutter rushed back in and made a whining sound;

He barked and shook and turned round and round.

Mud flew onto Ronnie's shirt.

"Where did you get all that dirt!"

Cutter ran back out the door.

Barking and barking even more!

Ronnie ran as fast as he could,

And followed his dog into the wood.

On the bank of the pond there was a clatter.

Ronnie got close to see what was the matter.

Fred the Turtle stood close by.

Ever so softly, Ronnie heard the cry.

Too much rain had caused a flood,

And two baby foxes struggled in the mud.

Cutter barked, and Mrs. Barnswallow chirped

While Fred the Turtle pointed to the dirt.

The baby foxes were sinking fast.

Stuck! The mud was thick and vast.

Ronnie waded up to his knees,

Then he pulled them out quick as you please.

Soon, the fox cubs were clean and warm,

Saved from the mud and the awful storm.

But finding their mother was a must!

Or the rescue might just be a bust.

Ronnie called the Fire Department. "What to do?"

"You must build a small den. You got a crew?"

"My mom and my dad, they'll show me how.

And my dog Cutter, he's my pal."

A cardboard box with a hole in the side

Put a board on the top. Not too wide.

A little bit of hay on the floor,

With food and water near the door.

The den was done, the fox cubs were safe.

He hated to leave them in that place;

But in the morning, their mom had come.

The babies were safe, he couldn't be glum.

The Fireman called him the next day.

He was excited and didn't know what to say.

They gave him a gold medal for being brave!

He left with a smile and a great big wave.

Cutter and Mrs. Barnswallow were friends indeed.

He couldn't have saved the fox without their lead.

They worked as a team just like he was taught.

He liked his teammates a WHOLE lot!

About the Author

Patty Wiseman lives in the deep woods of East Texas with her husband Ron and their dog, Cutter.

Because she is a grandmother and great-grandmother, she looks for stories that would inspire the children in her family. Nature surrounds her with many opportunities.

The story, Rescue at Wiseman's Pond, is an account of a real-life adventure. Saving the baby foxes inspired her to write the story for her grandchildren and great-grandchildren.

She is looking for other stories to share from deep in the woods of East Texas.

About the Artist

Syrena Seale lives in East Texas with her husband, their son, two dogs, two cats, a parrot, and a coop filled with dozens of chickens.

She is a graduate of Ringling College of Art and Design in Sarasota, Florida, and has illustrated a number of books and web comics. She is currently the director of concept art for Ferocity Unbound Core Studios, and is also a published novelist.

She eventually plans to create her own series of graphic novels.

CPSIA information can be obtained
at www.ICGtesting.com
Printed in the USA
LVXC01n0407151117
556026LV00003B/4